ISRAEL and PALESTINE

A JOURNEY THROUGH TIME – THE COMPLETE HISTORY FOR KIDS

Written and Illustrated
By

ALI WELCH

Long, long ago, in a land with golden sands
and ancient cities,
two groups of people lived. They are
the Israelis and the Palestinians.

These two groups
loved their land very much,
and they had many stories and memories
here. Each had their own special
traditions and celebrations

But just like in any story,
there were times when things got tricky.
Both wanted a place to call their own,
and sometimes they stepped
on each other's toes.

1949
1967
1973
1987
2000

Just like when two friends want the same toy,
they had disagreements. They both thought, 'This is my special place!

But, oh! There were times
when they tried to make peace

Leaders from both sides met, shook hands, and said, 'Let's be friends! They tried to make peace

Sometimes it worked,
sometimes it didn't

Just like a seesaw, finding balance was hard. One side up, the other side down, then switch!"

There were lines drawn, saying, 'This is mine, and that is yours.' But lines in the sand can be confusing and can change with the wind

As years passed, the story became even more complicated. There were moments of calm, but also unexpected storms.

In a place called Gaza, a group named Hamas took charge. They wanted a different future for Palestine.

Some countries, like Israel, the United States, the European Union, and the UK, called them a 'terrorist group'.

They disagreed with their methods and goals.

One day, a big surprise came from Gaza. Hamas launched a large attack on Israel, causing much sadness and fear.

Many people were hurt, and
some were taken away.

Israel responded, trying to protect its people.
They sent their soldiers, tanks, and planes.

But this meant more loud noises, more fear, and more tears for everyone.

Many kind-hearted people wanted to help and send food, water, and medicine.

But sometimes, it was hard to get these things where they were needed most.

In the middle of all this, everyday people, just like you and me, hoped for peace. They remembered the good times and wished for them again.

The United Nations, a big group of countries working together, called for a pause in the fighting. They wanted to make sure everyone stayed safe and got what they needed to survive.

Hamas had built many secret tunnels under the ground. These tunnels were like hidden pathways, and they played a big role in the story.

Many people had to leave their homes, searching for a safer place. Some went to cities like Khan Younis, hoping to find shelter

This chapter in the story was very challenging, with both sides feeling pain, loss, and fear. Just like a seesaw, the balance seemed harder to find.

But remember, in every story, even when things seem darkest, there's always hope. And just like before, many dream of a future where both Israelis and Palestinians live happily side by side.

These are sad times, with tears and heartbreak. But remember, even broken hearts can be mended with time, understanding, and love.

There are many who dream and hope. They wish for days filled with laughter, shared stories, and playing under the same olive tree.

This tale is still being written. And maybe, just maybe, when you grow up, you'll write the next chapter. A chapter filled with peace, love, and understanding.

Because every story, no matter how tricky, can have a happy ending. And all it takes is a bit of hope, a lot of heart, and friends who are willing to understand.